DEPTH
OF FIELD

DEPTH OF FIELD

Natasha Deen

orca soundings

ORCA BOOK PUBLISHERS

Published in Canada and the United States in 2022 by Orca Book Publishers.
orcabook.com

Library and Archives Canada Cataloguing in Publication
Title: Depth of field / Natasha Deen.
Names: Deen, Natasha, author.
Series: Orca soundings.
Description: Series statement: Orca soundings
Identifiers: Canadiana (print) 20210164298 | Canadiana (ebook) 20210164336 |
ISBN 9781459832206 (softcover) | ISBN 9781459832213 (PDF) |
ISBN 9781459832220 (EPUB)
Classification: LCC PS8607.E444 D47 2022 | DDC jc813/.6—dc23

Library of Congress Control Number: 2021934055

Summary: In this high-interest accessible novel for teen readers, Josh
discovers a criminal operation while on a photography assignment.

Orca Book Publishers is committed to reducing the consumption
of nonrenewable resources in the production of our books. We make
every effort to use materials that support a sustainable future.

Orca Book Publishers gratefully acknowledges the support for its
publishing programs provided by the following agencies: the Government
of Canada, the Canada Council for the Arts and the Province of British
Columbia through the BC Arts Council and the Book Publishing Tax Credit.

Edited by Tanya Trafford
Design by Ella Collier
Cover photography by Getty Images/Sandra Schmid
and Getty Images/in8finity

Printed and bound in Canada.

24 23 22 22 • 1 2 3 4

For Tabitha

Chapter One

The world is ending, and I can't breathe. Correction. My world is ending, and it's all thanks to Noel Brown. Noel and his weekly parties on his giant country property. Parties I never go to because Noel and I have a bad history. Like, Noel beating me up every day back in junior high.

But here I am, standing outside his house and looking through the window. I came tonight because my girlfriend, Lian, asked me to. Begged for us to go. Things have been rocky between us. I gave in. Told myself Noel wouldn't dare do anything. We're in twelfth grade now, and I'm over six feet tall. I tower over Noel. I thought, What's the worst that can happen?

And then the worst happened.

The window gives me a clear view of the living room and the couch. On that couch I see that deadbeat druggie Noel kissing Lian. Like, really kissing her, tongue and all. And it's painfully obvious that my girlfriend is totally into it. That's the part that crushes me. When was the last time she was that happy to kiss me? Come to think of it, when was the last time she kissed me?

"Hey, man, what are you, some kind of creeper?"

Someone claps their hand on my shoulder. It takes me a second to recognize my buddy Daniel. His gaze goes to the window. "Whoa, man. Isn't that Lian? When did you break up?"

I don't know, I want to say. "Uh…" I clear my throat. God, it feels like I swallowed a bunch of razors. "We didn't—" Sudden tears burn my eyes. I swipe them away and hope Daniel doesn't see.

Daniel springs forward and raps on the window. "Hey! Lian Wu, what are you doing?"

Noel and Lian snap apart.

"Josh just saw everything! Not cool!"

Lian's brown eyes go wide. She bolts upright. Her red-and-purple braid swings over her shoulder.

Noel leans back on the couch and smirks at the window.

It takes everything in me not to crash through the glass and punch him right in the mouth. Noel's been smirking at me since seventh grade. I hate that smirk. And I hate Lian for giving him another reason to think he's above me.

Daniel keeps yelling at the window, even though there's no way they can hear him. "If you're going to cheat on Josh, choose better than Noel! I've seen that dude kiss his reflection in the mirror." Then Daniel turns to me. He drops his voice. "I'm so sorry, man."

"Yeah."

Then Daniel goes quiet. That in itself is amazing. I've never heard Daniel go silent. That guy never stops talking.

It doesn't last long. "You and Lian should talk," he says. "Unless you need space?"

"From her or from you?" I ask.

Daniel grins. His teeth flash white in the moonlight. "Good one. Look, if you need me, I'm around, okay?"

I nod. As he steps back out of the bushes and heads around to the back of the house, I call out, "Hey, Daniel? Thanks."

"Yeah, man. It sucks, but it happens. Maybe you two will work it out." Then he's disappearing around the corner and heading toward the firepit at the back of Noel's property. And I head into a fight with the girl who used to love me.

Chapter Two

With every step, my feet feel heavier. Every passing second makes me feel old. By the time I step into the warmth of the two-story house, I feel like I'm a hundred years old, not seventeen.

My heart's wet and soggy. Maybe that's my face. I swipe at my cheeks again, then press my fingers against my eyes. How do I do this? How do I make her feel the total horror of what I've seen? Or maybe

I avoid the whole thing. Should I even say anything? Maybe I should pretend I don't care. Our relationship hasn't been great for a while. I could fake like she's done me a favor.

I spot them both in the hallway. Still together.

"I told you he wouldn't do anything," says Noel as they walk toward me. "He likes to believe he's a lover, not a fighter. But we all know what a coward looks like."

Now would be a perfect time for me to punch Noel. Or say something witty to prove I'm better than him. But that's the problem. In my head, I always defeat Noel. In reality, I do a weird frozen-rabbit thing. It's humiliating.

"I got this," Lian says to Noel. She leads me back to the living room where I saw her and Noel making out. There's no one else here. They must all be out at the firepit.

"Seriously?" I ask. "This is the place you pick for us to talk?"

"It's private," she says.

"Not that private," I mutter.

Her face goes bright red.

For a second all I can do is look at her. I loved playing with her hair. Loved how it would fall against her shoulders when she laughed. But she's not laughing now.

Neither am I. I look down at my hands. My skin's gone from brown to gray. I can't tell if that's because of the ceiling lights or if I'm losing color because my heart is bleeding out. I close the drapes. "How long have you been cheating on me?"

"This was the first time, Joshie—"

"Don't call me that. Don't ever call me that again."

"Don't be mad—"

"Don't be mad!" I yell. Oh god, she has me screaming. I lower my voice. "How would *you* feel?"

"Well, I guess I'd feel partly to blame," she says.

Seriously?

Her chin lifts. "I didn't do this on my own."

"No," I say. "You did it with Noel."

"That's not what I meant!" She sighs. "You played a part in this."

"*What?*" My eyes go wide, and I have to work not to yell again. "This is my fault?"

"Not all of it!"

Now she is the one screaming. I'm happy to see her losing control. To see her face go blotchy and red. For some reason it calms me. "Tell me," I say quietly. "How is this *my* fault?"

"You—we—" Her hands flap in the air. "You're boring, okay? Dating you is *boring!*"

Her words smash into the middle of my chest. I am no longer calm. For a second I can't breathe. "*Boring?*"

"Yes. We've dated for two years. You never do anything exciting. Noel's a risk-taker. He takes chances and lives on the edge. You know he jumped out of a plane?"

"Are you sure he wasn't pushed?" Usually, my being funny can break the tension when we're fighting. This time, the tension stays. Lian just stares at me, like *I'm* the one who did wrong.

"No one likes that guy, Lian!" I add. "I can't believe you cheated on me with him!"

Lian's eyes narrow into slits. "That's what bothers you? That I didn't choose someone you like?"

"My problem is that you did it! If you were so unhappy, why didn't you break up with me?"

"I didn't think it would happen, okay? We were just hanging out. He's so chill."

"No kidding," I say. "You know his folks are huge drug dealers, right? I bet he smokes half their stock."

"Don't say that." Lian's face tightens. "That's a terrible lie. Noel says it's not true."

"What else would Noel say? *Hey, Lian, yep, everything you heard is totally true. My family is* in 'the biz.' That's how we afford this huge place."

I shake my head. "His dad's an ex-con, Lian. He went to jail for growing pot. Everyone knows that."

"That was a long time ago. His dad doesn't do that stuff anymore. Noel promised."

"Two years together, but you choose to believe him over me."

She stomps over to the window. Then she whips around to face me. "I believe my heart."

I'm going to throw up. "What about your eyes and your ears, Lian? Everyone knows Noel's a user, and I'm not just talking about the drugs. He's using you for something."

Her eyes flash.

"Grow up," I bite out. "Not that. I mean for something else."

"That shows what you know." A satisfied smile crosses her lips.

Watermelon lip gloss, my brain reminds me. She wears watermelon lip gloss because it's my favorite. Correction. It was my favorite. It breaks me that she was wearing that when she kissed him.

"Noel's interested in my photography. He wanted to know all about our project for class."

I laugh. I can't help it. It seems unreal to laugh at the same time I feel like dying, and that makes me laugh harder.

"Stop laughing!" Lian looks like she'd like to throw a lamp at me.

But I can't. My girlfriend is cheating on me. My life's in pieces. But she and Noel were talking about school? It's too weird not to laugh.

"You're so petty! Don't you even care about what happened?"

Suddenly I'm not laughing anymore.

Suddenly we're screaming at each other. She's calling me names, and I'm yelling.

"At least I know to break up with someone before I go kissing someone else!"

"No you don't," she spits out. "That would take courage, and you don't have any! How long were you standing at the window watching us? I bet if Daniel hadn't said something, you wouldn't have done anything!"

It's true and it's not true. The blood rushes to my face, then speeds to my feet.

Lian's smile mocks me. "See? I was right. I can tell by the look on your face."

A hollow emptiness fills me. We're done as a couple. The girl I love doesn't love me anymore. "How did we get to this? Why didn't you just tell me how you felt?"

Anger drains from her face. For the first time, she looks sad. Lian shrugs. "I don't know. I tried." She gestures at the couch. "I didn't mean for this to happen. It was a mistake. It shouldn't have happened. As soon as I saw you—" She stops. Swallows. "I'm so sorry, Josh. I wish I could take it back."

"I'm going home," I tell her.

She reaches for her bag. "Sure, let's go."

That's when I remember she's my ride. Maybe I'll bum a lift with Daniel. "It's fine," I say, the fight gone from me. "I'll find my own way home."

"Don't be like that," she says. "We should talk."

Talking is the second-last thing I want to do. Being with her is the very last thing. "No thanks. Have a good night. Tell Noel thanks for a party I'll never forget."

I go looking for Daniel, but it's not easy. Noel's family lives on five acres just outside of Calgary. There's no cell service, so texting is out. I head toward the fire. All I see are shadows and half faces in the moonlight. I don't want to ask anyone where he is. Because then they'll talk to me. And I don't want to talk to anyone. I don't even want to talk to the voice in my head. Except to tell it to stop screaming and crying. *Just be quiet. Just shut up.*

I keep to the shadows because they hide my tears. My head's pounding, my throat aches, and I want to vomit. I'm about to give up and call a ride-share when I spot Daniel. He's by the firepit, arguing with a couple of the kids. I move toward him, but then someone grabs me and pulls me back.

Noel.

I take a breath. Prepare for the fight.

Chapter Three

Except it's not Noel. It's Lian's shadowy form in front of me.

"Come on," she says, sighing. "I'll drive you home."

"It's fine," I say. "I'll get a ride with Daniel."

"No," she says. "I want to talk to you."

In the dim light I can't see her face. But I hear the sadness in her voice.

"We were together for a long time," she says. "It sucks for it to end like this. I don't want you to hate me." There's a beat of silence, then, "I don't want it to end."

"I don't hate you." The words are easy to say because it might not be a lie. I'm pissed at her. I'm raging at Noel. But there's a part of me that thinks she's right. I *am* boring. I don't take chances. And let's face it. Lian was always out of my league. I still can't believe she even agreed to go out with me. My dads wouldn't agree. They would both say I'm "a catch." But that's parents, right? They always think you're number one.

"You're such a liar," Lian says, and I hear the laugh in her voice. "I can tell you're totally pissed off."

She could always tell when I wasn't being upfront. It hits, hard and fast, that all of this is gone. No more inside jokes or secret knowledge. "I'll get Daniel." My voice rasps.

"I can't make up for what you saw," she says softly. "Let me get you home. I screwed up. Let me try to fix this."

The wind picks up, ruffling my hair. It feels like it's going through my body too. I can't find the words to answer her.

She pulls at my sleeve. I let her lead me back to her car.

Neither of us says a word as she heads down Highway 1. She takes the off-ramp onto Highway 1A. The car is still silent.

I suddenly realize something. "Wait a second," I say. "You missed the turn for Stoney Trail." I rubberneck as the exit disappears from view.

"Finally," she mutters. "He speaks."

"You're the one who wanted to talk."

"That's why I'm taking the long way to your house," she says. "More time."

"Then talk."

"I didn't mean to call you boring." Her fingers tighten on the wheel.

"Yeah, you did."

Lian shakes her head. "It's just...everything was the same. Hang out with our friends. Go to the movies. Take drives around the city."

"I took the photography class for you. That's different." My head is throbbing again. I push the button to open my window. The air chills my skin. "If you wanted to do more, you should have said so."

"I didn't know what I wanted until Noel," she says. "He always makes me feel alive and appreciated."

And I don't, apparently. Then I replay her words. Realize she's talking about more than tonight. "Wait. How long has this been going on?"

"Tonight was the first time I kissed him."

Her words ring in my ears. That isn't really an answer. "I meant the hanging-out-so-he-could-make-you-feel-amazing part." My tone is sharp, accusing.

She glances at me before answering. "A while."

"Oh my god, Lian! So you're telling me that all the times you bailed on me, you were hanging with him?"

"Not all the time!"

"I can't believe this! You've been cheating on me for months!"

"I have not! I told you, tonight was the first time we kissed!"

I take a deep, long breath and resist the urge to scream. "You lied to me so you could hang with him. What would you call it?"

"Hanging with a friend. If I'd thought you'd be mature about it, I would have told you."

Is she saying she lied about cheating on me to protect my feelings? And I thought the night couldn't get any worse.

"You have history with Noel. I didn't want you overreacting," she says. "I know you don't like him."

"I *hate* him," I say. "That guy spent junior high stuffing me in my locker."

She gives me a fast side-eye. "I have the right to be friends with anyone I want. I knew you'd get weird about it."

"Of course I would! He's not a good guy!"

"He is! And I was being a good girlfriend by not dragging you into the friendship! What happened tonight was—"

"You're lying," I say. "You like him. You liked him when you were hanging out as friends. You didn't tell me because I'd have known there was more than friendship there." I'm not buying her "it just happened" crap. "Pull over, Lian. I'm getting out."

"Don't be so immature," she says. "You don't even know where we are. Grow up and let's talk."

Boring. Immature. I've had enough of her. "I know exactly where we are," I tell her. "We are at the end of our relationship."

"No—"

"Pull over!" I scream.

Lian jumps as the words echo in the car. She takes an off-ramp, speeds into one of the residential streets, then stops at the curb. She looks around for street signs. "I don't recognize these streets, Josh."

I yank off my seat belt.

"How are you going to get home?" she asks.

"None of your business." I unlock the door.

She locks it from her side. "Joshie, c'mon," she says. "It's late. Let me drive you home."

I unlock the door again and wrench it open.

"If you won't let me drive you home, let me wait," she says. "Call your folks and—"

"Goodbye, Lian."

"Don't do this! You have the worst sense of direction! This isn't safe!"

"I guess I'm not boring now, am I?" I slam the door and shove my hands into my pockets. Then I stomp toward a bus shelter and wait for her to leave. It takes a while. First she gets out of the car and starts my way. A few steps in, she changes her mind. She heads back to the car. Texts me. I ignore them all. Finally she leaves. Five seconds after she does, I realize I'm as immature as she said. It's freezing out here, no bus will be coming at this time of night, and I have no idea where I am.

I pull out my phone and check the map app. Half hour from home. I could call my dads, but they'll want to talk. Besides, it's their date night. My night's ruined. Why screw over theirs?

I use our family ride-share account and call a ride. Then I spend the time waiting freezing my butt off and being confused. Lian is right. I would have had a problem with her hanging out with Noel. But not only because he's been a jerk to me since forever. He's a user, period.

Noel doesn't do anything for anyone. Not unless there's something in it for him. And by something, I mean money, power or stuff. I huddle on the bus bench, trying to stay warm and trying to figure out why Noel's pretending to be Lian's friend. And why is he asking about our photography class? Eventually I give up. Let them have each other. Why should I care?

Still, it haunts me. When the ride-share arrives twenty minutes later, I still don't have any answers. Just questions. I can't help but worry about Lian. Noel is going to use her, then lose her. She's going to be devastated. Part of me feels happy about that part. The rest of me feels sad that I can be happy over her pain. I climb into the back of the car. My ears tingle with warmth. Spite turns back to worry. Noel is the ultimate bad guy. What has Lian gotten herself into?

Chapter Four

I see the lights in the family room from the street. Great. My dads are awake. Just what I need. I unlock the door and ease myself in, hoping they don't hear me. The sound of bullets and a car chase comes from the TV. Hopefully, they won't notice me.

My phone bings. Lian, asking if I'm all right. I ignore it and set the phone to silent. Then I head for the stairs. Baba comes into the hallway. Just my luck. There's a bowl of popcorn in his hands. "You never put in enough butter!" he calls back to Dad. Then he catches sight of me on the first step.

Confusion wrinkles his forehead. "Josh?"

"I'm going to bed," I tell him. "Good night."

But Baba's not having it. His dark eyes home in on my face. "Kwame," he calls out. "Josh is home."

I look away, embarrassed.

"Come into the kitchen," he says.

The noise of the movie stops. Dad appears in the doorway. He's wearing the same red flannel bottoms and gray top as Baba. It's corny how much they love wearing matching outfits, but tonight it hurts to see it. To know Lian and I won't ever have corny stories of our own.

There's no point in trying to pretend nothing's up. Both of my dads are mechanical engineers. They never leave a problem unsolved. I sit at the table and tell them what happened.

"What does this mean for your group project?" asks Baba.

I groan. What is it with South Asian parents and marks? My heart's a pile of broken pieces and all he cares about is my assignment.

Dad gives him the "not now" look.

Baba shrugs. "What? The kid's on the honor roll. That poetry class is bringing down his GPA."

"Photography class," I correct him.

"Whatever," says Baba. "You should have taken a class you're good at."

I make eye contact with Dad. "Is he trying to be helpful?"

Dad puts his hand on Baba's arm. "Dev," he says, then ups the volume on his "not now" look.

"What?" says Baba. "We can't let a broken heart affect his future."

I put my head on the table. This night is going from bad to worse.

"We can talk about that later," Baba adds quickly. "Right now we should talk about how you're feeling."

"I'm feeling like I want to go to bed."

They take the hint. Sort of. Neither of them can resist letting me leave without a long, tight hug. It's everything I can do not to fall apart. I pull away and head upstairs, wishing the night had never happened. Wishing I'd never met Lian.

Monday morning comes too soon. I sit at the kitchen table, stabbing at my oatmeal with a spoon.

"It feels good," says Dad as he comes into the kitchen, "but attacking your food will only do so much for a broken heart."

"Ha ha." I keep poking.

Dad knots his tie, then spins. "What do you think?"

"The pivot could use work."

"I meant the tie, Mr. Comedian."

The tie is lavender, and against his dark skin, it pops. "It's great," I say. "The client will love you." I return to stabbing my food.

"Stop that." Dad takes the bowl and spoons a mouthful.

"That's my breakfast!" I say.

"No, it used to be your breakfast," he tells me. "Now it's mine."

"I can't believe you're literally taking food out of your kid's mouth."

"If my kid ate the food," says Dad, "I wouldn't have to." He takes another bite and watches me.

Uh-oh. A full-on Dad lecture is coming. I stand. Hope I can get to the stairs before he opens his mouth.

"About this thing with Lian," he starts.

Too late for escape. I face him.

Dad clears his throat.

Double uh-oh. Whatever he's about to say, I'm not going to like it.

"Noel's not a good guy," he says.

"Tell me something I don't know." I shift my weight. Rock from one foot to the other.

"Lian's in trouble," he says. "We know her, Josh. It's not like her to do something like this."

"So what are you saying?" I ask. "I should forgive and forget?"

"No," says Dad. "But you need to talk to her. Find out what's really going on. She's a good person who made a mistake. And she's made it with a kid who—"

He stops. Anger flashes across his face. I know he's remembering all the times Noel bullied me and how the school did nothing. "I think you should look out for her."

Disbelief leaves me empty. Anger fills me up. "Are you kidding? She cheated on me, and you're choosing her side?"

"I'm not choosing sides—"

"It sure sounds like it," I say bitterly.

Dad comes over and puts his hand on my shoulder. "I'm not choosing her. I'm choosing my son. The part of him that looks out for the people he cares about, even when they make mistakes."

I try to shake him off.

Dad puts his other hand on my shoulder. "I'm mad at what she did. I'm furious. I hate that she's hurt you."

This time I shake him off. "Then how can you tell me to look out for her?"

"Because you're not just her ex-boyfriend," he says. "You're a human being in this world, and so is she. And she's getting involved with someone who can really hurt her." Dad's eyes soften. "It's easy to stand by people we like. Easy to stand by people who don't hurt us. But understanding ourselves comes from moments like these."

I can't believe he's putting this on me. Can't believe he's asking me to be the bigger person when he should be pissed at Lian.

"What's going on?" Baba joins us, fully dressed and holding his briefcase. "Let's go, Kwame. I need to get to the office early." He turns my way. "You want a ride, kiddo?"

I shake my head.

They leave—after another round of long, tight hugs. I rinse my dishes and head to the bus. I just have to get through the day, I remind myself. The worst has already happened.

⌒

I'm at my locker when I get the text from Baba.

Your dad told me about the talk in the kitchen. That wasn't fair of him.

Thanks.

He's right, but now isn't the time for it.

Thanks a lot. 👍

Find out what happens with the class assignment. I don't want your marks dropping.

Oh my god. Can someone give my parents sympathy lessons? Jeez. Like I don't have enough I'm dealing with. I send him another thumbs-up emoji.

"Josh."

I put my phone in my pocket. Mx. Mitchell is coming my way.

"We need to talk," they say.

I follow them to their classroom door. "Why?"

The teacher steps back into their room. "Lian turned in the group project," says Mx. Mitchell.

"Oh." I guess that's okay. We were mostly done anyway. No, wait. It's *not* okay. I was still editing some of the shots. I can't believe she did this without talking to me.

"Your name's not on it," they say.

"*What*? But we did it together!"

"You might remember," says Mx. Mitchell, "that I did warn you about the risks of partnering with your SO for a project." Mx. Mitchell is young but not *that* young. If they were, they'd know that talking in short form did not make them more relatable.

"She can't do this! Half those photos are mine, and I did the editing!" I mean, sort of. Lian helped me. A lot. The whole reason we took the class together is because *she* loves photography. I super suck at it. Oh man. If I screw up my GPA, Baba will have my head.

Mx. Mitchell folds their arms across their wool blazer. "You need to sort this out yourself, Josh." They move from their desk. "Today's Monday. You have a week to get the photo assignment in to me, or I'll have to give you an incomplete."

"But—!" I'm sure they know that Lian did most of the work. But I did help! That should count, shouldn't it?

"Next time choose someone you can work with. Don't just pick your friends. There are consequences to your decisions," they say.

"How was I supposed to know my girlfriend was going to cheat on me?" I blurt out.

Surprise, then sympathy flashes across Mx. Mitchell's face. "Not my problem, Josh." Their voice softens. "That's not even your problem. Your problem right now is the assignment."

"Maybe I can partner with another group?" I ask.

Mx. Mitchell considers it. Then shakes their head. "The groups are in the final stages of edits. It's not fair for you to share their marks when you haven't contributed to the work. I need to see what *Josh* can do. Show me something that tells me who *you* are. Show me what you can do."

The bell rings.

"All right, get to class," they say. Their face softens again. "And Josh? I know you're going through a hard time…"

I stare at them.

"Life is hard and mean and unfair," says Mx. Mitchell. "Part of growing up is learning how to push through and get the job done. Now, off you go before you're late."

I race for math class. I can't believe I thought things couldn't get any worse.

Chapter Five

Lunchtime, and I'm at my locker. I was going to text Lian. Ask her to get her stuff out of my locker. But now, after that stunt she pulled in Photography, I just want to dump her crap in the trash. The only thing stopping me is my parents. They'd be ticked if I decided to be petty. Especially given Dad's little talk this morning. Oh man. How am I going to tell them I have to start over with my project for photography class? Did I mention that Baba is going to kill me?

Damn Lian. Selfish, cheating Lian. Trying to keep my balance leaves me clenching my stomach. Who knew breaking up with your girlfriend would be a good core workout?

I want to rip off the photos, then tear them to shreds. But there are cameras in the halls. All I need is someone hacking the system, then posting videos of me losing my cool online. Lian would love that. So I peel off the photos. Carefully tuck them into my bag. God, my stomach's hurting. It's like I've eaten rotten food and guzzled a six-pack of soda, all at once.

"Hey, man, so I guess the talk didn't go so well."

I jump at the sound of Daniel's voice from behind me.

"Sorry." He smiles. "Didn't mean to scare you."

"How can a guy as big and tall as you not make any sound?"

That makes him laugh, because I tower over him. I go back to erasing every trace of Lian from my locker.

"I guess it's over?" He motions to all her stuff.

I tell him about the photo assignment. Instead of getting mad, Daniel's face lights up.

"That's great!" he says. "I just broke up with my group."

I'm lost. "Sorry?"

His lip curls back. "They were at Noel's party, when they were supposed to be working on their part of the project. We got into it at the firepit. They haven't done anything." The lip curl gets bigger. "They know how much it means for me to get a good mark. So they're doing nothing, letting me do all the work."

"That sucks, man," I say.

"Yeah, but now we can do the project together. I talked to Mx. Mitchell and ditched the whole group thing. They have to do a new project, and so do I. Let's partner up."

"I wish," I say. "But Mx. Mitchell wants me to do it solo. This is going to be one of those life-lesson moments they love."

Daniel makes a face. "Mx. Mitchell's cool, but yeah, why are they always trying to make us learn stuff about life and school? It's like they think they're a teacher or something." He grins.

I laugh.

"I'm going to go to Nordegg to get some shots of the wild horses," says Daniel. "Sure you don't want to join?"

That sounds awesome, and I'm tempted. Nordegg is a cool little spot a few hours from here. Not as busy as Jasper or Banff, but just as many trails to explore. And lots of photography possibilities. Then I remember Lian. How she'll sneer and say I just tagged along with Daniel.

He's doing the exciting thing, chasing wild horses. I'm just the boring friend who joined him. "That sounds cool, but I better do this alone."

"What are you going to do?" he asks.

"I don't know," I admit.

"Do you want to come along anyway?" asks Daniel. "It would be nice to have company."

"I can do that," I say slowly.

"Cool," Daniel says. "And think about what I said about working together. I bet we can convince Mx. Mitchell to let us pair up."

"Sure," I say, but I know it won't happen. Not just because of our teacher. If I hand in a project with Daniel and get a better mark than Lian, she'll say it was because of Daniel. It's petty to want to prove I'm better than her, but there it is.

Daniel takes off for the cafeteria. I shove Lian's stuff in a bag and take it to her locker. She's there, and I'm relieved to see she's alone. "Here." I hand her the bag.

She doesn't say anything.

"Thanks for this, Josh," I say, pretending to be her. "Super cool of you not to ditch my stuff."

She stays silent.

"Especially after I was such a jerk, you know, handing in our assignment without your name."

That gets her. She slams her locker door shut. Hard. "You want to talk about jerks?" She gets into my space. "How about forcing me to drop you off in a neighborhood you don't know? How about not letting me make sure you were okay? How about not answering my texts all night?" She blinks fast. "I was seriously worried about you."

"You don't get to be worried about me anymore!"

"Because of one mistake?" she says. "I told you, I'm sorry. I didn't mean for it to happen." She reaches out to me, then stops halfway. Her hand hovers in the air. "I'm sorry, too, about the assignment. I was just mad. I can talk to Mx. Mitchell."

"Forget it," I say.

"Well…how about if I help you?" she says. "The assignment is to take photos of nature and stuff. I know your mark isn't great—"

The idea that I need her help makes my skin burn. "I'm good."

"But—"

Now I'm super pissed. I can get a good mark without anyone's help. I hate her for thinking I can't do it alone. "Why don't you find Noel? Help him?"

"I'm sorry!" Her cheeks flush red with anger. "You know what? No. Forget it. I'm not going to keep begging you to forgive me."

"I don't want you to apologize," I say. "I want to know…why Noel? He's a user. He beats people up. He steals kids' money."

She must realize I'm asking it straight on because her face softens. "I know he's not a good guy to you—"

"Or anyone else."

"He's good to me," she says. "He asks about my day."

"So do I," I say, then correct myself. "So did I."

"Not lately," she says. "Noel…he likes hearing about everything. Even photography class." She laughs, embarrassed. "He asks about where you and I went to shoot our photos. The kind of equipment I use. He thought it was cool that we headed up to Nordegg just to explore the back trails. He thinks I'm awesome for taking photos of remote places hardly anyone will see."

I shake my head. "No, this doesn't make sense. Noel doesn't care about school. Why is he asking about that class?"

"Because I care about that class." The hard lines are back on her face again.

Back in fifth grade, Noel pulled the "let's be friends" act with me. Then I invited him for a sleepover. And he stole a bunch of my stuff.

When my folks tried to get it back, Noel's parents shut them down. There was a huge fight on their front lawn. Dad and Baba ended up buying me all new stuff. Which was cool. Except I couldn't look at any of it without thinking of how Noel had screwed me over.

I want to remind Lian of this, but she's already walking away. All I'm left with is a bad taste in my mouth. I'm positive Noel's going to mess her up. And I wish I could be the super-mature kid Dad thinks I am. But all I feel is glad. Glad that she's about to feel how I felt on Saturday night.

―

I spend the rest of the week trying not to throw up at the sight of Lian and Noel, everywhere I turn, joined at the lips. On Friday when the final bell rings, I book it to my locker. All I want is to be gone.

Just then Lian and Noel walk by.

"Noel," Lian says loudly, "you're such a great listener! Not at all like my last boyfriend."

Yeah, keep going, Lian. Noel's going to burn you, just like he did me.

Lian catches my eye and pretends to be shocked to see me. "Oh, Josh, I'm so sorry. I didn't know you were there."

"At my own locker?" I shoot her a look. "Yeah, right."

Her mouth twists to the side. She does that when she's pissed off. I used to think it was cute. It sucks that I still think it's cute.

"Where was that place we went in Nordegg? The one that was farther up the trunk road?" she asks.

"Why are you asking?" It's weird that she's trying to have a normal conversation with me. And it's not like she doesn't know the spot. She picked it. I slam my locker closed with more force than necessary.

Noel smirks.

Asshat. Can't he do anything else?

"I thought I'd take Noel," she says. "He's totally into my photography. I'm going to take him to some of the places we used to go to."

I shrug. What else can I do? Then I realize I should act all cool. That way she won't know how much it bugs me. "I don't know," I say. "We went off the trails, remember? Almost got lost."

She laughs. "I let Josh have control of the map," she tells Noel. "His sense of direction sucks."

It's a punch to the heart, hearing her laugh at me.

She gives Noel a playful look that guts me.

"I'm going to teach him everything I know," she says.

"That should take two seconds," I say. "If you talk slow." So much for pretending this doesn't bug me.

She flinches, and I walk away smiling.

"Off-trail at Nordegg?" I hear Noel say. "Sounds fun. How far off-trail?"

I grin at the idea of Noel wussing out on the rugged trails and paths. "I take it back, Lian," I say over my shoulder. "That far off the trails, it may take you *three* seconds."

"At least we'll have time for other things," she calls after me. "Unboring, exciting stuff!"

And I'm not smiling anymore.

An idea starts to burn in my brain. I'm going to show her I'm not boring. By the time I get home, I know exactly what I'm going to do for the photography project. And it'll prove just how exciting I can be.

Chapter Six

Saturday morning, and I'm in the kitchen. I've figured out what my topic will be for the project. Bears. It's totally *not* boring. I spent last night checking bear-photography groups. I have a list of tips and places to find mama bears and their cubs. Lian's going to eat her heart when she sees the shots I get. I text a note to Dad and Baba.

Heading out to Nordegg. Be home by eight.

I grab my gear. I've got snacks and water, my camera equipment and my phone.

"Josh?" Dad comes into the kitchen. He scratches his beard and squints at the microwave clock. "What's up?" I guess he hasn't seen my text yet.

"Flowers at sunset," I say and hope my face believes my lie.

Dad blinks again, then turns his squint to me. "Flowers at sunset? Is that code? Did you become a spy when I wasn't looking?"

"No, it's not code," I say, laughing. "The photography class, remember? I have to take some photos for my project. Daniel and I are heading to Nordegg." The best lies are the ones mixed with some truth. He knows about Lian handing in our project. I'll just let him think I'm working with Daniel now. I called Daniel last night and said I'd drive us up there.

"Oh! Right! Thank God," says Dad. "For a second I wondered if my blood pressure meds needed adjusting. Which flowers?"

Great. A total Dad question, and I don't have an answer. Damn. I should have figured he'd ask something like that. But I had bears on my mind. All I've done for the last twenty-four hours is search out how to find and take photographs of them. The online sites were awesome. They talked about bear scat and tracks. I'm going to nail this project. *Take that, Mx. Mitchell. And take that, Lian.*

"Not sure yet. I'm not going to pick only one," I say quickly. "I'm focused on the colors and stuff. I should get going. Don't want to miss the sunset. Bye." I need to get out the door and stop rambling. My palms are sweating so bad, I can barely grip my bag. I've never lied to my parents—not about big stuff, anyway. Lying about photographing bears is in the top five of Big Lies.

"Hold on. What time will you be home?"

"Eight. It's all in my text."

Dad's still squinting at me. This time his words are full of Dad sarcasm. "Yeah," he says, "but you're standing right here. Why would I read a text?"

I put my bag down. I need to give him time now so he doesn't worry later.

"To keep up your brain power?" I say. "I hear it helps you old folks."

"You're awfully mouthy for a kid who's borrowing my car," he says. Dad moves to the coffee machine and brews himself a cup.

"Sorry," I say. "You are the greatest of dads."

"Which trails are you taking?" Dad asks, ignoring my flattery.

"I'm not sure yet," I say. That part's true. "I thought we'd drive around and see."

"But you're not going anywhere remote or without cell coverage, right?"

I nod. That's true too. Mostly. I mean, if wildlife photographers are posting real-time locations online, it can't be that remote. Right?

"You're not going to be making any nimrod choices, are you?"

I roll my eyes. "No. I'm not going to make any *nimrod* choices. Okay, Grandpa?"

"I'm not sure I like this," he says. "Maybe I should come with you."

My heart jumps hard. I count to three before I say anything and keep my voice calm. "I'm not alone," I say to him. "Daniel will be with me."

Dad takes a giant gulp of his coffee. "But those back trails are remote. What if something happens?"

"But you let me and Lian go up there a couple of weeks ago!"

"Yes, and I didn't like it," says Dad. "I let Dev talk me into it, and I worried the entire time."

"Right," I say, "but if Baba says it's okay, then it's okay."

"Baba says a lot of things," says Dad.

"Like how well you're aging?" I grin.

The joke works. He grins back.

The moment gives me a chance to plan. If I put up a fight, Dad will push back. So I shrug and say, "If it's that important for you to come with us, fine. But honestly, I'm just going to be walking the trails taking photos of flowers and trees. I have to get the shots just right. You'll be standing around. A lot. And bundle up, because it's supposed to get chilly."

"How chilly?"

Another shrug. "I don't know…but it might be pretty windy."

My play is brilliant. Dad hates being cold. He shivers and holds the mug tighter.

"I guess if Baba says it's okay…" He stops. "Are you sure you're going to be okay?"

"Yeah, the trails will be fine. It's Saturday. Lots of people will be out."

"I meant about the breakup with Lian. You haven't really talked about it."

I pick up my bag. Pretend I don't feel the ice in my belly. "She made her choice."

He's silent for a bit. I know he's worrying about me. "You promise you won't be late?"

"I promise. I'm going to get the shots and then we'll come straight back. I'm going to be pulling all-nighters just to get the project in on time. I'll be home by eight. Eight thirty at the latest."

Dad studies me.

I try to look chill.

"Okay," he says, pulling me in for a hug. "See you later. Be safe."

I race out the door. Twenty minutes later I'm at Daniel's house. Then we're off and heading to adventure. *Take that, Lian!* Daniel talks the entire way there. About everything except my wreck of a love life. And I'm thankful for that. I'm glad I have a friend to fill the silence. I almost tell him about my plan to photograph the bear cubs, but I stay quiet. He'd talk me out of it. And I'd let him.

But I can't! I have to prove I'm not boring. I tell myself I'm proving it to Lian, but I know the truth. I'm trying to prove it to myself. So no way can I let anyone talk me out of this.

I park and we get our gear.

"Let's head this way," Daniel says pointing left.

I pull out my phone. I've memorized every tip the wildlife group posted about bears, but I read it all again. It doesn't hurt to be extra careful. After I lock the car door, I open my map app. I've pinned the locations where the photographers found bear families. The closest one is a twenty-minute walk. And it's in the opposite direction from where Daniel's pointing.

"I'm okay," I tell him. "I want to head on the other trail."

He doesn't look happy. "Josh, man, no. You could get lost in the back seat of your car. We shouldn't split up."

"I'll be fine," I tell him. "This site I googled mentioned a spectacular field of wildflowers up this way. I'd like to try to find it. I'm not going to do anything reckless, I promise." The lie slips easily from my mouth.

He nods slowly. "If you're sure..."

"Positive. Look, let's meet back here in a couple of hours, okay? I'll buy dinner."

Reluctantly Daniel finally agrees.

I race away before he changes his mind. I'm a few minutes into the trail and so focused on finding the bears that I don't hear the noise until it's too late. Something's coming up hard and fast behind me.

Chapter Seven

Panic blurs my vision. I turn around but am too scared to make out what's coming at me. Big. Wide. Fast. And talking.

Wait.

Talking?

"Hey, man." Daniel comes to a stop in front of me. "Are you *sure* you don't want to come with me?"

"Nah," I say, feeling irritated because he won't leave me alone. "I want to be different."

He laughs. "You're already there, my man."

"Shut up." I can't help but grin back.

"You want to walk together?" he asks. "We're doing different things, so Mx. Mitchell can't complain. But it would be nice to have company."

"Thanks, but Mx. Mitchell was pretty clear about me doing this on my own."

"At least we can scout locations together, right?" He looks to the sky. His eyes go unfocused. "Maybe I should do geese flying in formation." He tilts his face up. "Might be easier than wild horses."

"You should do your thing," I say, trying to keep the sharpness out of my voice. "And I'll do mine." I wonder if Daniel is nervous about being on his own. But if he tags along, he'll never let me go through with my plan. I need to get some space between us.

"What *is* your thing?" he asks.

"Flowers, I told you." I jerk my thumb toward the trail. "I should get going. I promised my parents I'd be home by eight."

Daniel's eyes flick toward the trail. He doesn't say anything, just stares at me for moment. "Josh," he says, eyes narrowing, "you're not planning to do something boneheaded, are you?"

"Like what?" I ask.

"I don't know. Jump in the lake? Maybe some kind of updated *Romeo and Juliet* thing? No poison. Just freezing your ass off."

I laugh, and he laughs with me. It feels good. "No," I say. "I'm not risking hypothermia for her."

Daniel nods. "So no other plans for something reckless?"

I try to come up with a lie.

He pounces on the silence. "Dude, you're cool and all, but you're a total wildlife novice. Please tell me you're not trying to track cougars or moose."

"What? No way!" Thank God he didn't mention bears. He knows when I'm lying.

"Good," says Daniel. "Because you know what they say about cougars, right?"

"They have a terrible sense of direction?"

Daniel's not laughing. "No, man. That the only time you'll hear one is when it attacks." He plucks at my jacket. "I don't like this, man. It's one thing for me to go off road. My family is all about back-trail hiking and remote areas. But you don't have any experience—"

"Dude, come on," I say. "I did the same trails with Lian, okay? It's nothing new or dangerous."

He sighs and gives in. "Okay, fine. But stay on the trails. Concentrate on the flowers, okay?"

I salute him. "Yes, sir."

He looks pissed. "Don't be a jerk about it," he says.

"Don't act like my dad."

"I'm not." He looks genuinely hurt. "I was acting like your friend."

Now I feel like the jerk. "I'm sorry, Daniel. Can I blame a bad breakup? I just need some space."

"Yeah," he says, finally cracking a smile. "You can." There's another pause. "Look, I don't mean to sound like your dads, but how about downloading the friend-tracking app?"

Damn. If I do that, he'll know immediately when I veer off the trail. And knowing Daniel, he'll try to stop me. "Ah—"

"Look, better safe than sorry, right?"

"Sure," I say. "Let's do it." We download the app, add each other and agree on a time to meet up.

"Good luck," Daniel says. "And Josh...don't be late."

I nod.

Daniel turns and walks away. And I'm this close— so close—to telling him we should just hang. I hate that I've lied to my folks and to him. But I have to do this on my own. After a while, when I'm hoping he's too focused on his photos to pay attention to the app, I delete it. Then I promise myself I'll be at the car waiting for him. He'll never have to know what I did. No one will. Not until I surprise everyone with the photos.

⌒

Pebbles and dirt scatter as I head down the trail. One of the photographers I found online marked a spot where they saw the bears. I'm searching for the first red ribbon that highlights the spot. As I walk, I'm wishing I'd had more time to plan this trip. I'm glad I brought water and food, but I could use a thermos of hot coffee. It's way colder up here than in the city. After I pull my tuque over my ears, I shove my hands into my pockets. My body urges me to walk faster, but I don't want to miss the marker.

After a while the sound of my feet on the trail starts to calm me. It's the *swish, swish* of my sneakers on forest floor. It almost sounds like the ocean. Sort of. Okay, not at all. But I'm alone in the woods. Despite all my efforts to ditch Daniel, I'm the one who's nervous.

I pull out my earbuds. Music can help, right? Listening to a favorite playlist will make me feel less alone. Just as I pop one of the buds in my left ear, I hear it. Something scuttling along the forest floor. I freeze. Where is the sound coming from?

My muscles go tight. My mouth goes dry. I listen. Hard. The sound doesn't come again.

It's just a chipmunk, I tell myself. I force my feet to take a few steps. *Or a squirrel.* Still, I duck behind some brush and wait.

Nothing appears.

I can't believe I was afraid of a chipmunk. Thank God no one's here to see what a rookie I am when it comes to the outdoors.

I stick my earbuds back into my pocket and keep going. My excitement picks up. The ribbon's supposed to be around the next bend in the path.

Sure enough, a hundred yards in, I see it. It's ragged and barely hanging from the tree trunk, but it's there. I hop off the trail and head toward it.

———

I'm sure I've been walking for a million years. I'm cursing out everyone. Lian for taking my name off the assignment. Noel for, well, existing. But most of all I'm cursing out myself. I am a Class A nimrod. A Class A nimrod who is 100 percent lost.

I remembered to fill the car with gas. And I remembered to bring food and water. Too bad I didn't remember to download the compass app.

Too bad I didn't remember to take screenshots of the map so I could get back to the car. I take out my phone. Again. I lost the cell signal a while ago. Still nothing. That means no downloading the compass app. No calling for help.

"C'mon, Josh, think!" I tell myself. I must know something about how to get back to the trail. I pull up the notes from the bear-tracking sites. At least I was smart enough to screen-shot them! I check the instructions. Find the first ribbon. Check. Walk a mile west. Cool, except which way is west?

"Come on, come on!" *And stop talking to yourself.* I scan the sky. The sun rises in the east and sets in the west. Great. Except the sky is overcast. There's no sun to find.

A group of geese flies overhead. Man, I wish I'd gone with Daniel. I'm going to die in these woods, and no one will ever find my body. The fear and tears rise, but I shove them down. Feeling sorry for myself won't help.

Geese fly south for the winter, right? I face the direction they were coming from. It's not winter anymore, so the geese are on the way home. Let's say I'm now facing south. Then west is on my right side. Ha! I knew I could do it! I pivot and go looking for the second ribbon. Then all I have to do is take photos of the bears and retrace my steps.

Easy peasy.

Except...it's not. After another half hour, I still have no idea where I am. Every step is cold, sharp and miserable. I can't believe it. I'm totally lost in the wilderness, and I have no idea how to get out.

Chapter Eight

I spend a few minutes cursing myself and my ridiculous plan. Again. Then I take a breath. I have to get out of here. I have to get home. My dads will kill me if I die.

Okay, I'm lost in the mountains. What should I do? Peeing my pants comes to mind. But that's not a helpful idea, so I throw it away. I also throw away cry, scream and run around in circles.

I need to be smart, and smart takes energy. Eat. I should eat something. Wait. I should ration my snacks, then eat something. I sit on a rock and take out a protein bar. Sitting lasts for two seconds. The rock is cold and freezes my ass. I stand and eat. Then have to stop myself when the bar is half-finished. I'm surprised how hard it is to stop eating. Surprised to find myself hungrier than I thought.

I guess being a nimrod and getting yourself lost takes more energy than I thought. I put the bar back in my bag. I walk in a circle around the rock to keep my body temperature up.

Then it starts to snow. Not something I'd usually expect at this time of year, but it happens up here.

Great. Just great.

Hang on a second. This *is* great! Falling snow means snow on the ground. And that means footprints. I will be able to see if I'm doubling back on my path. Even better, I can see if there are other footprints! I can follow them to safety.

To be smart—for once—I grab a branch. I can swish it to the side when I walk. That way I'll know if the tracks I see are mine. I grin. I'm a genius.

Just then a coyote's howl echoes through the trees. A moment later there's a returning howl.

I'm not grinning anymore. I'm back to being the nimrod who's about to be coyote or cougar food if I don't get out of the mountains. I check my phone. No signal still, but I've got a full battery. But that won't last if I don't keep the phone warm. I tuck it in my front pocket. After making sure my pack is zipped back up, I speed off in a straight line.

Wait. Maybe walking fast in the snow and the cold isn't the smartest thing to do? Maybe I should slow down? Conserve my energy? That seems like a good thought. You know what's another good thought? That I should have taken survival class instead of photography. Wait, that's a useless thought.

Is thinking useless crap a sign of hypothermia?

The snow's coming down in bigger flakes now. Luckily it's drifting snow. That's good news. It means my footsteps won't be covered up too quickly.

Maybe it's the cold. Maybe it's the sound the snow makes as it falls. I've never noticed there's a swish as it brushes against my coat. Maybe because I've never been quiet enough to notice. It's silent enough to shove some hard truths into my mind.

About Lian. About how ridiculous being in love has made me. What made me decide getting photos of a bear and her cubs would prove anything? Jeez. What a way to go, trying to prove a point to a girl who chose a loser druggie over me.

I need to stop thinking. All it's doing is making me want to cry. And that will make me give up. I need to keep going. Even if my hands are cold. Even if the wind stings my cheeks. Even if my toes are so frozen, it's hard to walk.

I stop and check my phone again for bars. None. But the battery is holding. Good. If I'm still out here when it starts to get dark, I'll need the flashlight. I need a better plan than wandering aimlessly and looking for a signal.

Oh! As soon as I can get a signal, I'll phone Daniel. If I can't get him, I'll try 9-1-1. Maybe they can get me help. Then I'll download the compass and a map app and get myself out of this park. After that I'll find out if witness protection covers nimrods. I'll need it. When my parents find out what I did, I'll need someone to protect me. I glance at the phone. I'm surprised to see I've been out here for only two hours.

Daniel is going to start worrying if he sees I've deleted the tracking app. But maybe if I can find my way out of here soon, my dads will never have to know what I did. If I can get my brain in gear, I can get back to the car. Then maybe even Daniel won't have to know either.

The ground rises under me. I'm heading for a hill. Good. Hills are higher ground. Maybe I can get a cell signal. There's a buzzing in the air. I look up. A drone!

Sweet! Where there's a drone, there has to be people! Maybe I can get into camera range and wave the operator down for help. The drone disappears over the hill.

I'm halfway up the hill when I hear an electric sound. It's like the faint hum of a generator. Double sweet! Maybe these folks are glampers. I'm imagining a hot fire and good food. Imagining myself entertaining them with my story of getting lost.

Farther up the hill I hear voices. I stop. Hear the sound of my breath. The painful pounding of my heart. Hope makes it beat hard. I start toward the sound and then panic as the voices fade. Retrace my steps and try again.

And then...there! I can hear them louder now! I crash through the bush, then force myself to slow down. I'm sure cougars don't live in trees, but I'm no expert. All I know is I don't want to be dinner just when I'm almost saved.

Still, I can't help but rush. I run toward the voices. The wind stings my face, but I don't care. I keep going. I get to the clearing. In front of me is a patchy field of red flowers. In the flowers is a group of people. Behind them is a couple of trailers. The kind that construction guys use for their offices.

Saved! I'm saved!

I rush forward. I trip over my feet and crush the flowers. I'm not going to die!

"Hello! Hey there!"

The group turns. There are four men. They seem startled by my appearance. I can't blame them. I'd be spooked if some kid came running out of the trees, screaming.

"I'm so glad I found you! I'm so lost!" I'm grinning and waving.

They're not waving back.

They're not grinning.

They're reaching into their pockets.

Even in the gray light, I can see what they're pulling out.

Knives.

They're pulling out knives and coming for me.

Chapter Nine

My survival instincts kick in. I spin the other way. Then I'm off and running. I don't know what I've walked into. I don't care. My brain is screaming, "Big guys with weapons! Run! Run! Run!"

Their voices are behind me, and I run harder. Bounce into a couple of trees. Trip over some roots like the doomed victim in a horror flick. Fall hard and fast. But I'm up and running again. I'm too freaked out to feel any pain.

The men's voices are closer. So close, I can hear them.

"Spread out!" shouts one. "Get him!"

His words would be funny if my life didn't depend on it. What else does he think his men are going to do with me? Play a weird new game of tag?

Daylight's starting to fade. Good. It hides my footprints in the snow.

The sun's setting. Bad. It's getting harder to see where I'm going.

I fall again. Scrape my hands against some rocks. Instinct makes me grab a handful. After I scramble to my feet, I'm running again. And making enough noise to scare off any cougars that might be nearby. I chuck some rocks to my left. Chuck the others to the right. Hoping the sounds will hide my true location.

"Go left!" one man yells. "You! Go right!"

It's working.

Or he's tricking me.

No time to wonder.

I dodge around the trees. My lungs burn. My legs burn too. There's a harsh sound following me. It takes me a second to recognize it. Me. Crying. Sobbing. My breath coming in ragged, broken gasps. I grab more rocks, but they're getting harder to find. I'm grabbing and chucking. And trying not to vomit.

I break through the trees and stumble into the open. It's a stream, surrounded by pebbles. I can't run along its banks. I'm too exposed.

I can't go back.

The men are coming my way.

There's a row of trees on the other side of the water. I can hide in them if I cross the stream. But how deep is it?

No time to consider that. No choice but run into the water.

Time to sink or swim. I have no other choice.

—————

The water's freezing. It's so cold, I almost back out. But icy legs are better than dying in a forest. Dying without anyone ever finding out what really happened to me. I force myself to keep going.

The water comes up to my knees, but it doesn't get deeper. I race to the other side and dive into the bank of trees. I hide behind a tree. Pretend my jeans aren't clinging to me. That I'm not shivering. My teeth chatter, and I can't stop it. But when two shadowy figures emerge from trees on the other side of the stream, I hold my breath. I shrink and try to make myself invisible.

The figures run to the water. Then stop. Look around.

I can't hear what they're saying. One waves his hand to the left. Then waves to the right. They split up and start walking. They don't go into the water.

I can't believe it.

I got away.

For now, says the voice in my head. These men know these woods. What do I know about the wilderness? Nothing.

I fumble for my phone. As long as I have battery power, I can call 9-1-1. Except I can't find my phone. It must have fallen out when I fell. The tears and the panic explode, but I shove them down. I can't lose it now. Maybe I'm wrong. Maybe I still have my phone. I dig around in my bag. I check all the pockets in my coat and my jeans. Nothing.

Oh god. Nothing.

I don't have a phone. No help. No flashlight. No hope.

Maybe I can cross the water again. Maybe I can find it where I dropped it. Except there are at least two men waiting for me on the other side.

Even if I could get back to the trees and keep away from them, the sun's sinking fast now. And I don't know where I fell. Don't know where I ran.

Panic turns to terror. It takes over my bones.

What if the other men find my phone? All my information is on it. They'll know where I live. They'll find my dads. What will they do to my parents to find out about me? Because now I know I must have stumbled onto something very, very bad. Something those men will be desperate to keep hidden.

What have I done?

The thought of something happening to my family does something to me. I'm still freaked out. But I can't let those guys win. I don't know why they're chasing me. I have to get back to the car. Have to get home.

I have to get away from the men, but it's snowing again. That's when I remember the branch trick. I can brush my prints away. I check the ground for broken branches that have leaves. Anything I can use to hide my tracks. It takes a few precious seconds, but I find one. I'm brushing at my tracks, trying to make them disappear.

That's when I see it.

Bear scat. Great. Just what I need. I've run from the terrifying men and straight into bear territory.

Chapter Ten

I'm frozen in place, staring at the scat. Wishing I'd never decided to photograph bears. Wishing harder that I wasn't such a nimrod. Wishing hardest that I'd done more research. There are too many questions crashing around my brain.

Is the bear still around? Maybe it left? I hold my breath and listen. Everything's quiet. Except my heart. That sucker's pounding so hard, it's going break my ribs.

I laugh at myself, then take a breath. I need to concentrate on what I do know.

There are two kinds of bears in Nordegg. Black bears and grizzlies.

What else? It's spring, which means the bears will be...what? What does that mean? That they're well fed and less likely to attack me? I don't know! What I do know is that between the bears and the humans, the men are more dangerous. Which means the men are the ones to focus on.

Okay, one question answered. Some of the tightness in my chest relaxes.

Next question. How do I get away from the men?

The light's almost gone. That's good, I see now. The snow's not too thick, and that's also good. I scan the trees, looking for one with low, thick branches. There's one about twenty steps away. Squinting into the dark, I step carefully. I go to my tiptoes. Step on roots and exposed rocks. That way I don't leave footprints.

Slowly I get to the tree. By the time I touch the trunk, I'm ready to scream. I'm so freaked out. I'm terrified the men will find me. Terrified the bears will find me too. I force down the panic. It's not going to help me.

The branch is just out of reach. I jump and grab hold. Then I haul myself up. So far, so good. I take the next branch and pull myself up. It's a strong branch and should hold me. As I climb onto it, a few smaller branches break off and fall to the ground.

Damn it. They're going to give away my location. I keep going, but slower. And it's killing me. Time is slipping by. There's no way these guys won't find my prints. No way they won't be able to track me down.

It's getting colder now too. My fingers are frozen. The skin on my face is starting to sting. I keep climbing because there's nothing else I can do. My bag gets caught because the branches are closer together.

I cling to a branch and slide one arm free. Then I do the same thing with the other arm. I find a branch that can hold the bag. After I make sure it won't fall, I start to climb again. Then I reach back and pull up the bag. I keep going, higher and higher.

The cold is turning my pants to ice. I can't stop shaking. I can't feel my toes. But it's good, I lie to myself. Being cold is good. When I start feeling warm, that's when I know I'm in trouble. Being warm would mean hypothermia has set in. Which would mean I'd lose fingers, toes, a limb or my life.

When I have climbed as high as I dare, I sit on a branch, hold tight to the trunk and go still.

Just in time.

Through the branches, I see lights.

The men are coming.

Chapter Eleven

They're still far away, but their voices carry. I can't hear what they're saying, but I know they're pissed. Two of them are arguing. The wind carries bits and pieces of their conversation.

"...unbelievable!" says one of them. "...one job!"

"...I...fix...!" says the second guy.

"Can't...right!" The first guy's getting more pissed off.

"...found him!" The second guy's words come through loud. Clear. And *totally* pissed off.

I don't move. I couldn't even if I wanted to. My jeans are frozen to my legs. My fingers are too cold to bend or unbend. They're locked in a clawlike grip on the tree. The men get closer, and the arguing is louder.

I'm trying to put together their words, add it to what I saw in the field. If I can do that, I can figure out why they came after me. But nothing makes sense. A stupid field with flowers. It's not like they were burying a body or murdering someone.

The wind brings the smell of cigarette smoke. Oh god, they must be close now. A few seconds later the beams of the flashlights light up the ground.

"Two nosy kids can ruin everything," says the first man. "I'm holding you responsible if this goes down."

Two kids? Did Daniel run into them too? My body flashes hot. The heat burns and makes my fingers throb. Did they get Daniel? Did they hurt him? I press my hand against my mouth so I don't scream. If they hurt him, I'll never forgive myself. I should have joined him. We should've just taken photos of geese or horses and been done with it.

If I get out of this, I promise—

"Two nosy kids?" asks the second man, interrupting my prayer. "Don't you mean three nosy kids? Or did you forget about him?"

There's a moment of silence. One of the beams of light jumps, then falls. Someone's dropped his flashlight. There's a muffled sound. The second flashlight falls to the ground. Someone groans. Another muffled sound. Another groan.

They're fighting. The first man must have punched the second. I keep listening. He keeps punching.

I'm crying, and I don't try to stop the tears. If this is what the first man does to a friend, what will he do to me? It feels like the beating goes on forever. There are new sounds added. The first guy kicking the second. I try not to throw up, but the vomit keeps rising in my throat.

"Don't talk about my kid like that," says the first man.

There's silence. The beating's stopped.

"If it weren't for him," says the first man, "you wouldn't even know what happened. You're lucky I don't kill you." There's a final kick. "Some security guard you are."

One of the lights from the flashlight bobs and moves across the ground. The first man picks it up.

Slower, the light from the second flashlight moves across the ground. The second man is getting to his feet and picking up his light.

"Find the kid," says the first man. "Fix it."

They're talking, but all I hear is "fix it." *Fix it. Fix it.* Those two words echo in my head.

There can be only one way to "fix it." I'm going to die tonight. I'm going to die because I wanted to prove I'm not boring. What a stupid reason to die. My throat closes up. I can't breathe. My fingers claw at my throat. I punch my chest, trying to jump-start my lungs. It doesn't work.

I can't believe my luck. These guys won't have to kill me. I'm going to suffocate up in a tree. Then I'm going to drop at their feet. A gift to them, from me and my ego. It's funny and horrible all at once. Regret twists my insides. So hard, it makes me gasp. I take the breath. Go light-headed at how good it feels to get air in my lungs.

A third light flashes across the forest floor.

I start holding my breath again.

"Did you find him?" The third man is breathing hard, but his voice sounds familiar.

"No," says the first man.

"I told you," says the third voice. "He's not a threat."

And it hits. I know that voice! It's goddamn Noel!

Wait.

Why is Noel here?

"Josh is such a loser, I bet he doesn't even know what he saw," says Noel.

I almost come out of the tree. Almost launch myself at him from the branches.

"Anyone with two brain cells would know what he saw," says the first guy.

Noel laughs. "Exactly. Josh barely has one brain cell."

The good thing about Noel being here is that I'm not cold anymore. My fury burns hot. The other good thing is that Noel has me breathing again. I'm not worried about suffocating anymore.

There's a scuffling sound. I brace for the man to punch Noel, but I don't hear any thumping or groans.

"Don't be a wise-ass," says the man. "We're in real trouble."

"I'm telling you," says Noel. "Josh doesn't have a clue."

I really want to punch him. God, I hate this guy. Especially because he's right. I don't have a clue.

"Let me handle it," says Noel. His voice oozes with slimy confidence. "I'm sure he's heading back to the trunk road. I can take care of him." He laughs. "I've been taking care of him since sixth grade, Dad."

Dad! It's a blinding flash. My confusion burns away. The flowers were red. Poppies are red. Poppies make opium and heroin. That's what they're doing in the woods. Growing poppies to rebuild their drug-dealing empire.

Noel's dad laughs. "Okay, you do it."

The three of them walk away. Three flashlights move into the distance. Then one falls to the ground, but the group keeps moving. Their voices fade into the darkness. I stay quiet and still until the voices are gone.

Even then I don't move. Not until I'm sure they're gone.

Once I'm safe, I climb down. It takes a long time. My joints hurt, my legs are sore, and my fingers are clumsy. I get to the ground, then check to make sure I'm still okay. The night is silent. I move to the flashlight. I'm going to use it to double back across the stream and try to get to safety.

I'm bending down to pick up the flashlight when I hear him.

Noel. Laughing.

He steps out from the shadows. "You're so easy to con," he says. "Don't you ever get tired of being such a loser?" He reaches into his backpack and pulls out a knife. "No sudden moves, right? We're going for a walk."

I raise my hands and step away from the flashlight.

Chapter Twelve

Noel waves me away.

"I told Dad I could handle you," he says. "And I was right."

"Big words for a guy with a knife," I tell him. "I could handle you, too, if I'd come with weapons."

"Did you even bring bear spray?" he asks. "Of course you didn't. You have no idea how to take care of yourself in the wilderness." He gestures to my bag. "You didn't even bring bells."

I'm surprised into asking, "Bells?"

"For the wild animals," he sneers. "To warn them you're around."

Being mocked by Noel is bad enough. Being educated by him is worse. I'm tempted to tell him to stab me and be done with it. Luckily, my ego has learned its lesson. "What did you do with Daniel?"

His face slackens with surprise. Noel covers it with a smirk. "Took care of him, didn't I?"

Nice try, but I'm not buying it. So he doesn't know about Daniel. Which means my friend is safe. It also means that the two kids the men were talking about are probably me and Lian. "That's why you tagged on to Lian, isn't it?" I say. "Because you heard us talking about the trunk road?"

He nods. "Had to make sure you weren't coming near us."

"We wouldn't have," I say.

"You just did!" He shakes his head like I'm the biggest loser.

"Only because I got lost." I'm babbling, but he doesn't seem to care. Good. As long as I can keep him talking, I have time to figure out what I can do. Fighting him for the knife will get me stabbed. Noel's been a bruiser since he was a baby. No way can I win in a full-on fight. Still, I'm holding my own, and that counts for something. "Anyway, what's the big deal? You don't have enough poppies in the field to do anything." Yeah, right. Like I'd know.

"You're such a loser," Noel sneers. "That's what the trailers are for. Controlled environments for the plants."

"You're not going to kill me, are you?" I try to sound pathetic. It's not hard.

He shrugs. "We'll see what the old man says."

"But we know each other!" As if that matters. This is the kid who flushed my head in the toilet. A lot.

Noel shrugs again. "We'll see." He waves at me to start walking.

I point to the flashlight. "You want to get it, or should I?"

"Go for it," he says.

I pick it up and light the way. Noel doesn't say anything about my holding it. Good. Maybe I can use it as a weapon.

Trust Noel to be a mind reader. "If you're thinking you can use that light to fight me," he says, "think again."

I am thinking again. And I'm going to keep thinking until I have a way to get myself out of this.

"When we off you, we can make it look like a bear attack," Noel says cheerfully. "It's not hard. Drizzle your body with some honey and it's done."

He's trying to freak me out. It's working. My palms are sweating so hard, I can barely hold on to the flashlight.

"Is that how you want to go? By bear?" he asks.

I don't say anything. I won't give him the satisfaction.

"Maybe we should do cougars," he says, enjoying the moment.

My legs buckle under the thought. I cover it up by pretending to stumble over a branch.

"Lian is right," Noel says. "You really are useless."

I pull my sleeves over the flashlight. It helps my grip, but it can't help my vision. It's getting harder to see. Not only because of the darkness. It's knowing I'm walking into the worst moment of my life.

They won't kill me. They can't. I bet his dad beats me up and tells me to stay quiet.

Except I won't.

They must know that.

Oh god. I'm dead. I'm so dead, and Noel is going to be the one who does it. I swipe at my eyes. My foot gets caught in a root. This time the stumble's real.

Noel grabs me from behind.

I feel the wicked point of the knife at my back.

He shoves me down and kicks me. Hard. A surge of nausea rises. I can't stop it. It spews out.

Noel swears and jumps out of the way. "Gross! Get up! Let's go!"

I stand. My body sways as I wipe my mouth.

"Go!" He shoves me, and I stumble ahead. The light catches the thick trees and the stream in the distance. Every step brings me closer to his family. Closer to my end. My brain still can't wrap itself around reality. It's still shouting that things can work out.

But how?

Noel would kill me, bring me back to life, then kill me again. And he'd do it just for the fun of it.

"On the bright side," Noel says, his good mood back again, "I'll make sure Lian is okay."

I don't say anything.

"She was really happy to dump you, wasn't she? Don't worry. She and I will be real happy together."

And it's too much. I've put up with him chasing me, mocking me. Put up with him laughing about the ways he'll kill me. Adding Lian is too much. For the first time since Noel pulled the knife on me, my brain's clear.

I keep walking, looking for a tree root. When I see one that's big enough, I take my chance. I trip and fall. Toss the flashlight to the side. Before Noel can get to me, I say, "Sorry! Sorry!" Then I crawl toward the flashlight.

I figure Noel will like that. Me, on my hands and knees, scuttling away from him.

He laughs and proves me right.

I take hold of the flashlight and stand. As I do, I fling it at him.

Instinct makes Noel put up his hands, and it's all I need. I rush him, hard and fast, and drive him into a tree. With anyone else, it would knock them out. All it does is piss Noel off. The flashlight's rolled away, leaving us in semidarkness. It's enough for me to see he's dropped the knife.

I scan the ground for it, but Noel's coming at me. He lunges for me. I try to dodge away, but the snowy ground is wet and slippery. I go down, and he's on top of me. For a small guy, he's heavy. And possessed. He's punching hard and fast. Noel slams his fist into my ribs. My jacket gives me padding, but it's a solid hit. It steals my breath. But I'm not going down.

I grab his coat and twist my body.

Noel's not having it. He grabs my head and slams it into the ground. The sky disappears in a cloud of black.

He laughs.

It brings back all the times he laughed at me. All the times he beat me up, shoved me into the lockers and stuck my head in the toilet.

Rage takes over. I grab him by the neck, shove his head back. He's surprised. I'm bigger and stronger than he remembers. I use his shock to push him off me.

Noel's on his feet and crouching in a fighting position. "Who knew you had it in you, Joshie?"

I scream and run at him.

He dodges out of the way, but I reach out, wrap my arm around his waist. I swing him around and fling him into a tree. Noel bounces off. He's dazed, shaking his head and trying to find me.

I don't give him the chance.

I run at him and punch him as hard as I can.

He goes down. And this time he stays down. I gasp, wincing because every breath is agony. Noel doesn't move. I grab the two phones and his keys, and I run. One of the phones is a satellite cell. I dial 9-1-1 and start crying when the voice on the other end says, "This is 9-1-1. What's your emergency?"

"My name is Josh Biswas," I say. "I'm lost in the wilderness by the trunk road in Nordegg. I've stumbled on a grow op, and the men running it are trying to kill me." I start bawling. "Please, I need help."

Chapter Thirteen

I use the GPS on the phone to navigate my way out of the woods. The 9-1-1 operator stays with me the entire time. I'm surprised that by the time I reach the parking lot, the cops are already there. I spot Daniel in the crowd of officers. We make eye contact, but I don't get a chance to talk to him. That's probably good anyway. He looks wildly pissed off at me. I guess that's for making him worry when I didn't show up.

I feel bad for that. But watching Noel, his dad and their crew get hauled into the cop cars makes me feel better. I take a ton of pictures and decide I'll use them for my photography project. Mx. Mitchell wanted wildlife, right? Can't get much wilder than Noel, can it?

I get checked out by the medics. Then I give the police all the information I have and hope they'll let me go.

Shows what I know.

They take me to the cop shop, where they phone my dads. While I wait, I see Daniel by the vending machine. I head over, but he's already walking out the door. I text him. No reply. I decide to let it go and wait for him to cool off. By tomorrow he'll understand, I tell myself. We'll be good.

What's not good is the look on my parents' faces when they get to the station. It's enough to make me wish I was still lost in the woods. Almost.

"I can't believe you, Josh! I just can't believe you!" Dad yells as we head to the car. He keeps yelling the same sentences all the way home.

Baba doesn't say a word. That's scarier.

After the longest car ride ever, we finally get home.

"How much trouble am I in?" I ask Baba as he closes the door.

He doesn't answer the question. Instead he says, "Fix a plate, then go to your room. Don't come out until we call you." He blinks hard and tries not to cry. "I can't begin to tell you how disappointed I am in your choices."

I don't grab any food. I've lost my appetite. I go straight to my room, but I don't sleep. I spend the night listening to the rumble of my dads' voices and feeling like the worst kid in the world.

They come to me the next morning. First there are the questions. Why did I lie to them? Do I understand what could have happened? Do I know how lucky I am that I made it out alive?

I answer the best I can, but I know that no answer will be good enough. Nothing I can say will explain what I did. They ground me for three months. No going out, no TV, nothing but school and home. I take the punishment. I deserve it. I wait for them to add more. The worst part is seeing their disappointment.

"We love you, Josh," says Baba. "I hope you know that."

Dad nods.

I tear up. They hug me. Hard. I hug them back. It doesn't change what I did, but it tells me that things will get better. Eventually they'll forgive me.

By Monday it's all over the school. Everyone knows about the grow-op bust because it's been on the news. The media named Noel's dad, so kids know it was his family that's been charged. The news talks about how the grow op was discovered because of a lost hiker. That's me. But they don't name me or show my face because I'm in high school. So how does everyone know it was me?

I keep my head down and root around my locker. Pretend I don't hear kids whispering. Pretend I don't catch them pointing at me. Pretend I don't see school security cleaning out Noel's locker. I guess he won't have time for school if he's fighting jail time for the grow op.

Daniel, ever silent, appears from nowhere. "How mad are your folks at you?"

"Wait a second," I say. "Are you the one who told everyone that I'm the lost hiker?"

He shrugs. "I went with you to the cop shop, remember?"

"How could you do something like that? It was my private business!" I ask. Well, yell. I yell at him.

Daniel's eyes go wide and angry. "How could *I* do something like that? What about you? You lied to me! You could have died out there!"

"I had it handled," I say. "I survived. In case you didn't notice, the cops were waiting when I got out of the woods. You know why? Because I called them."

Daniel's face goes red. "You didn't call them. I called them. When you didn't meet me back at the spot, I checked the app. You weren't showing up. I got scared, so I got help. That's why the cops and rangers were there when you got back. Because of my giving them a description of you and hoping you hadn't died in the woods!"

And it hits me. What a terrible friend I was to him. He was honestly worried and looking out for me, and I shut down the app. "I'm sorry," I start to say, but he doesn't want to hear any of it.

"Forget it." He scowls. "Just forget it."

"No, Daniel! I made a mistake. I let my feelings get to me, okay? I'm sorry. I didn't mean to screw with our friendship." I'm talking, but my brain is exploding. I'm saying the same kind of stuff Lian said to me. And I wonder if her insides twisted the way mine are right now. Daniel's face mirrors the betrayal I felt that night with Lian. "I won't do anything like that ever again," I say. "I learned my lesson."

"Whatever, man," he says. "I got to go. I'll catch you around."

I deserve him walking away. Just like Lian deserved my walking away. But now that I'm the one who is wrong, it's a weird life lesson. I grab my bag and head to Mx. Mitchell's class.

They're waiting for me at their desk.

"I uploaded my photos, just like I promised," I tell them.

Mx. Mitchell nods. "I saw. Photos from the grow-op arrest. I heard you were the lost hiker who notified the cops."

I shrug. "Sort of. Daniel called the cops before I did."

The teacher's eyes go wide with surprise. "Daniel was with you?"

"Not really." I tell them about meeting up with him, the app and all the brainless stuff I did because I had something to prove to the world.

"Let me get this right," says Mx. Mitchell. "You—a wildlife rookie—went to the back trails to take photos of bears."

I nod, humiliated.

"You got lost, and then, by some weird twist, stumbled onto the grow op that Noel's family owns," Mx. Mitchell continues.

I nod again.

"You know, Josh, I wasn't sure about the grade I was going to give you," they say, "but now I'm positive. You deserve an F. If I could grade you lower than that, I would."

"What? That's not fair!"

"You want to talk about fair?"

"Look at the photos," I say. "They're good! And I worked hard for them. I was almost killed for them! My dads have grounded me for three months. I'm not allowed to do anything but school. I should at least get a good mark for this!"

Mx. Mitchell stares at me. "Let me put this to you another way, Josh. You risked your life doing something you shouldn't have been doing—"

"But—!"

They hold up their hand. "You shouldn't have been out there. You didn't know what you were doing. Your actions were selfish and rash. Did you think of what could have happened if you'd stayed lost? Did you even consider how your parents would have felt?"

That hits hard. When they were grounding me,

both Baba and Dad had been crying. Not just because they'd almost lost me. But also because I'd lied to them. I'd broken their trust in me. I shuffle in place, unable to meet Mx. Mitchell's eyes.

"That's what I thought," they say. "And what about the bears? Did you even consider what it meant to trespass into their territory? Did you even care about what would have happened, not only to you but to them, if there had been an encounter?"

I feel so small. I never once thought about the harm to the bears. "I'm sorry," I say.

Mx. Mitchell was not done. "And did you ever, ever consider the source of the information you were getting online? Real wildlife photographers don't post the location of the animals because it's dangerous for the animals. Josh, you're so lucky you didn't get hurt or worse!" Their voice shakes.

Mx. Mitchell is another person I let down. "I'm sorry." God, I'm saying that a lot today.

"You did all this to prove a point to your girlfriend, didn't you?" they ask.

All I can do is nod.

"You know what's really sad?" Mx. Mitchell asks. "You're a good person. You're a good friend. You never needed to prove anything to anyone."

I blink back the tears. "I get it. I understand." Baba is going to kill me for the F, but I realize I deserve it. "I'll see you in class."

I head for the door. I'm almost into the hallway when the teacher calls me back.

"Josh," Mx. Mitchell says. "A lot of the groups didn't do well on this assignment. I'm going to give everyone one more chance. Then I'll use the higher mark of the two projects."

I feel air enter my chest again. "Thanks. Uh, how about if I do something with the honey farms just outside the city? If I can get permission from the farm owners?"

They give me a small smile. "Sounds safe. Sounds good."

I head into the hallway and find Daniel.

"I'm still totally pissed at you," he says. "But I hate being pissed at you by myself. Want to hang out and I'll just glare at you?"

My chest relaxes a little more. "Yeah, that sounds good." I tell him about the new assignment and ask if he wants to join me. "You can glare at me, scowl, yell—whatever you want." I blink fast. "As long as you hang with me, I'm cool."

"Yeah," he says. "That sounds good. Especially the yelling part."

We head to the class, and I spot Lian by her locker. She sees me. Turns her head away.

"Hey, Lian," I say.

After a second she spins my way. Her face is hard. She folds her arms across her chest. She's braced for me to make fun of her because of Noel. "What?" she says.

"Daniel and I are hoping to photograph the honey farms this weekend. Do you want to come along?"

Lian stares at me. "Seriously?"

"I'm still totally pissed at you," I tell her. "And I don't know what happens next. But…let's just say, I know what it's like to make a choice you regret."

She slowly lets her arms drop to the side. "Seriously?" she says again.

"I'm pissed at him," Daniel tells her. "And he's pissed at you. Somehow it balances out."

Lian laughs like she's not sure about any of it.

"Sure, why not?" she says finally. Then she steps in between me and Daniel, and we head to class.

Acknowledgments

I'd like to express my gratitude to the Orca pod for all their hard work on this project. From the meetings on cover art, formatting, and the myriad other things that go into publishing a book, I'm thankful for their work and care on Josh's story. I'd also like to extend an extra thanks to Tanya Trafford, editor extraordinaire, for her keen insights and amazing catches when it came to revising the story. Lastly, to my readers. I know you can choose any book. Thank you for choosing mine and spending time with Josh and his adventures.